2 BEARS DELIVERY SERVICE
ALWAYS ON TIME
SCHEDULE
MONDAY
TUESDAY
WEDNESDAY
THURSDAY
FRIDAY

TRAIN OFF THE RAILS with Kody and Dot

Copyright © 2016 Green Toys Inc.

Art Direction & Storyboards by Brian Gulassa
Book Design by Iain R. Morris
Produced by Cameron + Company
www.cameronbooks.com

ISBN: 978-0-9971434-0-9
Lot# 0323180509
SKU# BKTN-4340

Printed in the USA

Green Toys Inc.
4000 Bridgeway, Suite 100
Sausalito, CA 94965
www.greentoys.com

TRAIN OFF THE RAILS

with Kody and Dot

Written by Robert von Goeben

Illustrated by Mike Yamada

Kody and Dot are delivery bears,
who drive a delivery train.

Day after day, around the loop,
their job is always the same.

They load up the boxes onto their
train, then drive around the bend.

Drop off the boxes, go back home,
and start all over again.

No special trips or different plans, always the usual way.

Same train, same route, the same little loop. Every single day.

When Kody and Dot first started their job, they never fussed or complained.

Kody would guide their way on the map, and Dot would drive the train.

But after a while, they needed a break. Was this the only way?

Same train, same route, the same little loop. Every single day.

The loop was small but it was tricky,
as Kody's map would show.

The hills, the corners, and lots of bumps,
"Dot, please take it slow!"

But one afternoon, when deliveries were done,
the train bounced a little too high.

They hit the big bump, the train took a jump,
and flew right into the sky.

CRASH went the train,
through very tall bushes.
Not in the usual way.

And right off the tracks
went Kody and Dot.
Not an average day.

"The train is OK," said Dot in a worry. "But how will I know where to steer?"

Kody said back, "We're off the map!"
But soon it was perfectly clear.

In uncharted land, with no map or plan, Dot had a carefree smile.

"Our deliveries are done, let's go have some fun and drive off the tracks for a while!"

Kody didn't know. "Where will we go?
And how will we ever get home?"

"Just add to the map," Dot said back,
"Let's wander a bit on our own."

So wander they did,
as they steamed on ahead.
There was just so much to see.

Boats and planes and hard-
working trucks, and wait...
What could that be?

One of their boxes on top of a boat,
and one on top of a plane.

Wow, just look, those were the boxes
that came from the little bears' train!

But nothing prepared them for what came next, as they steamed on past the lake.

Over the hill, came such a big thrill.
Dot pulled the lever to brake.

Were those the boxes they loaded that day?
Did they really come this far?

But there they were, strapped on top of every truck and car.

"This is amazing," Kody exclaimed.
"I thought that our job was so small."

Dot agreed, "I know what you mean.
It is a big job after all."

After a while, Dot said with a smile,
"The sun is getting low. We should get back
and find our track. Just tell me the way to go."

Kody had marked every turn
on his map. Every left and right.

And before they knew it, their
little loop, was coming back
into sight.

One final jump, and back on the track,
the way they'd always known.

And on his map, one final note.
Kody marked it "HOME."

Kody and Dot now see their world
in a much more wonderful way.

They deliver their boxes,
and then they explore.

Every single day.